DATE DUE		

Relatively Speaking

Poems About Family

by **Ralph Fletcher**

drawings by
Walter Lyon Krudop

Orchard Books
New York

For my family and relatives:
you gave me nothing less
than laughter, love,
roots, and story—R.F.

To my family—W.L.K.

Orchard Books, A Grolier Company
95 Madison Avenue, New York, NY 10016

Manufactured in the United States of America
Book design by Mina Greenstein
The text of this book is set in 11.5 point Janson.
The illustrations are black-and-white line drawings.
10 9 8 7 6 5 4 3 2 1

Library of Congress Cataloging-in-Publication Data
Fletcher, Ralph J.
Relatively speaking : poems about family / by Ralph Fletcher;
illustrated by Walter Lyon Krudop. p. cm.
Summary: A collection of poems that describe the experiences
and relationships in a close-knit family.
ISBN 0-531-30141-9 (trade : alk. paper).—
ISBN 0-531-33141-5 (lib. bdg. : alk. paper)
1. Family—Juvenile poetry. 2. Children's poetry, American.
[1. Family life—Poetry. 2. American poetry.]
I. Krudop, Walter, date, illus. II. Title.
PS3556.L523R45   1999   811'.54—dc21   98-30238

CONTENTS

Relatively Speaking

Being the Youngest

I'm eleven—youngest
one in the family.

There's Mom and Dad
plus my big brother,
God's Gift to Girls.

He likes to call me
el bambino
and junk like that

but he's the oldest so
what would he know?

Nobody expects me
to act like an angel,
to be super polite.

Nobody's surprised if
I act spoiled, if I take
the last piece of cake

and that's the way
I like it.

My Big Brother

Explained to me
        about Santa Claus,
showed me how
        to light a match,
taught me
        my first curse.

Now he's sixteen
        obsessed with friends,
girls, cars,
        lifting weights
and I'm nowhere
        on that list.

My Brother's Girlfriend

She's amazingly cute but
what could she possibly see
in a kid like my brother?

They stop over the house
on the coldest winter day,
two hickeys on her neck.

Mosquitoes are awful bad
this time of year, I tell her
and she makes a face at me.

Inheritance

My friend says he's going to inherit
a million bucks from his old man
when he kicks the bucket.

We're not rich or even close to it
but I'm curious so I ask Dad
what I'll inherit from him.

He says: *You can have my warped big toes
or my hairy ears, go ahead,
take your pick.*

I say the hairy ears to keep me warm.
I definitely don't want his warped
sense of humor.

Teamwork

Even in winter Dad makes me
wash the cars every Saturday.
I ask him: *Why can't we go to
the car wash like everyone else?*

Dad says: *A family is a team
and even teams like the Bulls
with the greatest superstars
know how to work together.*

Oh yeah? I ask. *So where's my
million bucks, huh? Where's my
championship ring?*

Here, he says and throws me a
sponge.

The Bravest Deed

I'm shopping with Mom
at the supermarket
and we see a woman
yelling at her kid who
looks about three or four.

> She grabs the girl's arm
> smacks her on the bottom
> *BANG! BANG! BANG! BANG!*
> about ten times, hard, then
> *CRACK!* across the girl's face.

> > The girl is screaming
> > and the lady gets ready
> > to smack her again
> > but all of a sudden Mom
> > sort of steps between them
> > and asks: *Is everything okay?*
> > *You're having a hard time,*
> > *looks like. I remember…*

> > > Mom points at me, laughing,
> > > actually calms the lady down
> > > with that girl still sniffling
> > > and me standing there hoping
> > > no one will notice my
> > > trembling hands.

Mom Drops a Bomb

We drive home from the store.
Mom says: *Wait a sec,* so we sit
breath steaming up the windows.

I want to tell you something
she says, dead serious, and
I start to feel a little worried

but she says: *I'm three months
pregnant,* and looks embarrassed
like she's too old for a baby.

I have to say something so I
mumble, *Hey cool,* and notice
outside it's starting to snow.

What Other Families Eat for Lunch

For lunch Mom serves sandwiches: P-B-'n-J
or maybe grilled cheese with chowder,
or tuna fish with pickles and chips,
or, once, crabmeat sandwiches
but that was a special treat
I don't expect we'll
see again soon.

My friend Sal
invites me to his house.
They ask me to stay for lunch—
his mother serves steaming ravioli
a huge bowl of it plus fresh garlic bread
so delicious I scarf down seconds and thirds
then she brings out this huge platter of cold cuts:
pepperoni mortadella these cheeses I've never heard of

and the next day at home it's pretty hard going
back to Mom's P-B-'n-J sandwiches
with chips.

Habits

We do have a few strange habits
in my family like the way
we fix corn on the cob.

First we butter a slice of white bread
and fold it around the corn
hot-dog style.

Trust me: you won't find a better way
to get your corn nice and melty
(plus you get to eat the bread).

At restaurants we have to fix our corn
like all the other normal families
using knives to spread the butter

every one of us secretly wishing for
slices of white buttered bread
so we can do it right.

Glass Flowers

Grandma takes me out
to a museum with these flowers

you'd swear must be real
but they're made out of glass.

A guy invented the formula
but never told it to anyone else.

He made them so beautiful but
took the secret to his grave.

Grandma's face is lined
like a map to buried treasure.

She must have secrets to tell
if only I knew which
questions to ask.

Part of the Wind

It's snowing hard.
I sit with Grandpa
drinking tea
and playing pitch.

I ask if he feels
like an old man;
he cuts the cards
and looks at me.

When I was a kid
                    we had a big hill
and I'd run down
                    with the wind
at my back.
                    I'd feel it lift me
and I became
                    part of the wind.
I can't do that now.
                    In the mirror
I see an old man,
                    but I remember
  when I was
                    part of the wind.

Broken Ice

A kid falls through the ice
which is bad enough but
this is even worse
because the kid is
my brother.

He was skating with his girlfriend
when the lake ice gave
                                              way.

He was in the icy water
almost twenty minutes
unconscious by the time
his friends pulled him out.

I drive with Mom to the
hospital. Dad's out of town.

The doctors say scary stuff
                    say *collapsed lung*
                    say *hypothermia*
                    say *critical condition*

His girlfriend cries and says:
I'd just broken up with him,
says it over and over
like it's all her fault.

The Story

They put him on a
respirator: a machine
to help him breathe.

In the waiting room
outside Intensive Care
Mom pulls me close
like a favorite quilt
and tells the story
in a whispery voice
of when I was born.

Bedtime

Sometimes I remember
the good old days

sitting on the kitchen floor
at night with my brother

each on our own squares
of cool linoleum.

I'm fresh from the bath,
wearing baseball pajamas.

Outside the screen door
summer breezes stir.

Mom gives us each two cookies,
a cup of milk, a kiss good-night.

I still can't imagine
anything better than that.

King for a Day

My brother is much better.
He's off that awful respirator
and home from the hospital.

He barks orders from his bed.
Get my book. Coke, no ice.
Get the CD I left downstairs.

Usually I don't let anyone
boss me around like that
but right now I don't mind.

Today I'll let him be king
just because he's breathing
on his own again.

Grandma

On the first warm morning
she's kneeling in the dirt,
smiling and humming
like she does making bread.

Grandma's planting tulip bulbs
that are almost the same color
as her own worn knuckles.
Watch how her hands work

the dark mounds of soil
in that dirty confusion
of bulb and knuckle,
knuckle and bulb.

The Scar

I'm playing war
with six of my friends,
using sticks for guns

arguing over who's dead
who's only wounded
who can die the best

when the door opens
and Grandpa walks out
wearing no shirt.

We see the scar
on his back. He got it
in a real war.

Nobody says anything
but after he passes by
we start a different game.

The Family Plot

Whenever we go visit
Grandma and Grandpa
we always have to visit
a certain old cemetery.

Dad slowly steers the car
past the granite gravestones
while me and my brother
crack jokes in the backseat.

The family plot is on a hill
overlooking a stone wall.
Nice view, my brother says.
Good drainage, I put in.

Dad turns to stare at us, hard.
Grandpa says: *I'll be buried
right next to my sweetheart*
and Grandma smiles at him.

There's room for us all, Mom says
and the cheery way she says it
makes it sound like we'll be
camping underneath the stars.

My Father the Comedian

We're having a reunion,
relatives from all over
gathering in a big house
on a lake way up north.

Dad tells my brother and me:
*I guarantee that this will be
the wildest party of the year,
relatively speaking*

and laughs at his own dumb joke.
Dad isn't even a little bit funny
but he thinks he's hysterical
which really cracks me up.

How About an El Drinko?

How about an el drinko?
my uncle asks first thing
when he shows up.

He fixes himself a drink,
Scotch-on-the-rocks

gulps Scotch after Scotch
and finally falls asleep
on the living room couch
snoring like a chain saw
cutting down some
faraway forest.

We talk around him
like nothing's wrong
and my uncle becomes
one of those lost men
sprawled on the sidewalk
everyone pretends
not to see.

Mom's Big Brothers

Mom has three big brothers,
big guys with thick arms
and beer bellies.

They mug for a picture
with Mom in the middle
and they all look pregnant.

My uncles talk loud and swear
but you can tell how much Mom
loves it when they tease her.

Today she seems more like
my uncles' little sister
than my mom or Dad's wife.

Precious Linda

Uncle Pete comes
to the reunion
with his new wife
Eva from Peru who
hugs everybody
but makes by far
the biggest fuss
over my cousin
Linda
who has mud-brown eyes
fat marshmallow cheeks
string-bean hair
until Eva washes it
puts in rows of neat braids
tied off with silver ribbons
saying over and over:
Mi Linda preciosita,
and kisses the small girl
whose face blooms
into such a smile
she looks almost
beautiful

Boy or Girl?

At the family reunion
everyone wants to feel,
poke, stroke, and admire
Mom's swollen belly.

The hot question:
boy or girl?

Let's vote, my aunt says
and polls the whole group:
fifty-one vote girl
forty-six vote boy.

Funny thing about babies:
nobody wonders about
blue eyes or brown,
bald or hairy,
short or tall,
big or small,

so why does BOY or GIRL
matter so much?

Melanie

My big cousin Melanie
looks at me and waves.
She took care of me
at another reunion
when I was four
and the grown-ups
went out fishing.

My cousins had found a squid
washed up on the beach
dragged it back home
in a big metal basin.

Later playing tag I
forgot about the basin
and fell back into it
felt cruel squid arms
pulling me under.

I screamed
and kept screaming
till Melanie pulled me out.

She wrapped me in a towel
and put me onto her lap
and stroked my hair
and wiped my tears
and I told her:
I love you.

She looks at me now
with a smile that says
she won't bring it up,
and I won't, either.

Cousin, Once Removed

The relatives are doing a puzzle,
one of those thousand-piece jobs

but I'm picturing my cousin Tim
eleven years older than me,
a kid who told the wildest stories
and knew almost everything.

I could never tie a square knot
till he showed me a shortcut.
Keep your knots loose, he said,
if you hope to untangle them.

But last year he got into trouble,
cut himself off from the family,
moved somewhere out West.
Nobody talks about him now.

When the puzzle is finished
my cousin Linda yells out:
We're missing one piece!
and I know which piece it is.

We Don't Talk About That

We're eating and talking
getting louder and louder
piling words onto words

until I bring up the time
Uncle Frank went to jail
and Dad bailed him out.

The talking stops.
I picture a dungeon,
an iron door bolted shut.

Later Mom tells me:
We don't talk about that

as if that explains
everything.

Singing

We don't sing too much at home.

At our house we sing together
only on someone's birthday.

It's different at these reunions.
At night Dad builds a bonfire
while my uncle tunes his guitar.

Pretty soon everyone's jamming:
Beatles, Diana Ross, James Taylor,
Jailhouse Rock, If I Had a Hammer,
Bye-Bye Miss American Pie.

Singing by this blazing fire
I feel like we're a clan, a tribe,
connected by blood and song.

Family Photo

One last picture
before we head off
in different directions.

One last group shot of
all of us, smirking,
with rabbit ears.

Three generations,
kids on shoulders,
a baby cousin on my lap.

And in the middle
Grandma and Grandpa
who started all this.

We're all ripples in a pond
spreading out
from a stone they threw.

Shrink-wrapped

We leave the reunion, go home
to a house that's much too quiet.

No more tag or kick-the-can or
killer croquet with my cousins

no more bloody war stories
from my big-bellied uncles

no more staying up late watching TV
while the grown-ups crazy-laugh
around the kitchen table.

Just us. Boring us.

Our family becomes
like a package of plums
shrink-wrapped
at the supermarket

so small and tight
I can hardly breathe.

Artist at Work

Mom brings out paints and brushes.
She's working in the baby's room,
painting rainbows and rain forests
and bright parrots on the walls.

She's wearing an old smock,
cranking the radio, singing along,
listening to oldies, windows open,
painting monkeys and elephants,
horses, hippos, hummingbirds,
zebras, sunsets, waterfalls.

I think she's getting carried away:

Next I'm going to paint the ceiling,
clouds with the major constellations,
and I'll work lying on my back like
Michelangelo in the Sistine Chapel.

Beach Muscles

My big brother is pumping iron,
doing curls and sweaty squats
in a corner of the garage.

But when Mom asks his help
to lift some rugs in the basement
he moans: *Whoa! That's heavy!*

and that makes Mom laugh.
What are these for? she asks,
grabbing his biceps.

These aren't for work, he says.
*These are beach muscles;
you know, just for show.*

Summer Chores

My brother has to cut the grass
water all the shrubs and flowers
but he usually skips the flowers
so he can sneak off to the beach
until one day he takes a shower
singing like a rock 'n roll fool and
doesn't notice his elephant feet
clamped over the drain so the water
overflows all over the bathroom floor
leaks through Dad's just-painted ceiling
starts a spectacular   w
                                    a
                                    t
                                    e
                                    r
                                    f
                                    a
                                    l
                                    l   in the hall
and makes a small lake that spills out
onto the front steps and t
                          r
                            i
                              c
                                k
                                  l
                                    e
                                      s

down to the two rosebushes so I say:
At least you watered the flowers,
genius.

New Boss

Mom asks if I'm looking forward
to having a new baby so I tell her:

> *It'll be nice to have a rugrat*
> *that I can boss around.*

She says we'll need new rules
with a new baby in the house.

> *Infants need a ton of sleep.*
> *Learn to walk on silent feet.*

Which makes me wonder just
who will be bossing who?

At the Beach

At the beach
I see a man
in the distance
all silhouetted
so much sun
behind him I
can't see his face
though I could
tell who he is
even in my sleep
the tilt of that walk
the sloping angle
of that not-so-
perfect posture.

When I yell: *Dad!*
he looks up at me
moves closer and
by strange magic
grows back his hair
loses thirty pounds
looks young again
with muscled legs
until I realize it's
not my dad at all
it's my big brother
kicking sand at me
saying: *Better get
some new glasses.*

The Turtle

I remember something.
It happened on the beach
years ago with Mom and Dad.

We were walking along a jetty
when we saw a gigantic turtle
wearing seaweed and barnacles.

It had crawled onto the rocks,
huge and green and hurt real bad,
its head flattened. It moved slow
like it was in pain. Dad told Mom:
Better take him back to the car.

She led me over granite boulders
with dark caves underneath
and lots of clear tide pools
hissing in and out.

I climbed into the backseat
trembling with awe and fear
but feeling proud of my dad
who would do the right
hard thing.

Standing Together

At my uncle's funeral
the old church is packed:
aunts, uncles, second cousins,
grandparents, nieces, nephews.

The priest says: *Please stand*
and we rise like one person.

Some days they make me crazy
but I know one thing: they will
stand with me, no matter what,
and I will stand with them.

Stopping Traffic

Folks hardly notice us
when we go out for a walk

but at a wedding or funeral
there are so many relatives

it's like I'm part of an army
clacking down the church steps

surging toward the street
overflowing the sidewalk.

The traffic waits a long time
till we've all crossed over.

Time

Driving home from the funeral
we're talking about my uncle.
I guess his time was up, Dad says.

Mom leans back, hard, and moans.
I guess mine is too, she whispers
and we detour to the hospital.

New Baby

Soon as the baby gets born
before she's two hours old
people start dividing her up

"She has Daddy's big ears"
"Got Grandma's double chin"
"She has my olive eyes"

like she's just a bunch
of borrowed parts
stitched together.

Well, I just got to hold her.
I touched her perfect head
and I'll tell you this:

My sister is whole.

Being a Middle Child

You got promoted,
my big brother says.
Guess I can't call you
el bambino anymore.
I think I'll call you
the peanut-butter kid,
stuck in the middle,
surrounded by bread.

I say he can call me
whatever he wants;
I'm going to love
being a middle child.

Dad and Mom will be
so busy with the baby
plus keeping track of
my brother's social life
they won't have time
to crack down on me
and I like it that way.

Asleep at Last

The baby cries so much
she's driving us crazy.

Mom and Dad try this and try that
but the baby keeps screeching

screaming howling wailing weeping
for a hundred years or longer

and just when we're about
to blow a family gasket

falls asleep.

We shut off the phone.
We take off our shoes.
We talk in sign language.

(Shhhhh!)

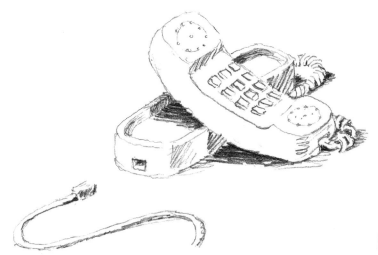

Grandpa

When the leaves turn colors
Grandpa comes to visit
and we go hunting arrowheads.

Did you know that your ancestors were archers,
makers of fine bows and arrows?
It's true, you know.

They fitted feathers onto their arrows
to make them fly straight
and strike true.

I tell him archery is pretty cool
but I want to be a writer
when I grow up.

Well then, he says, *what feathers will you use*
to make your words fly
straight and true?